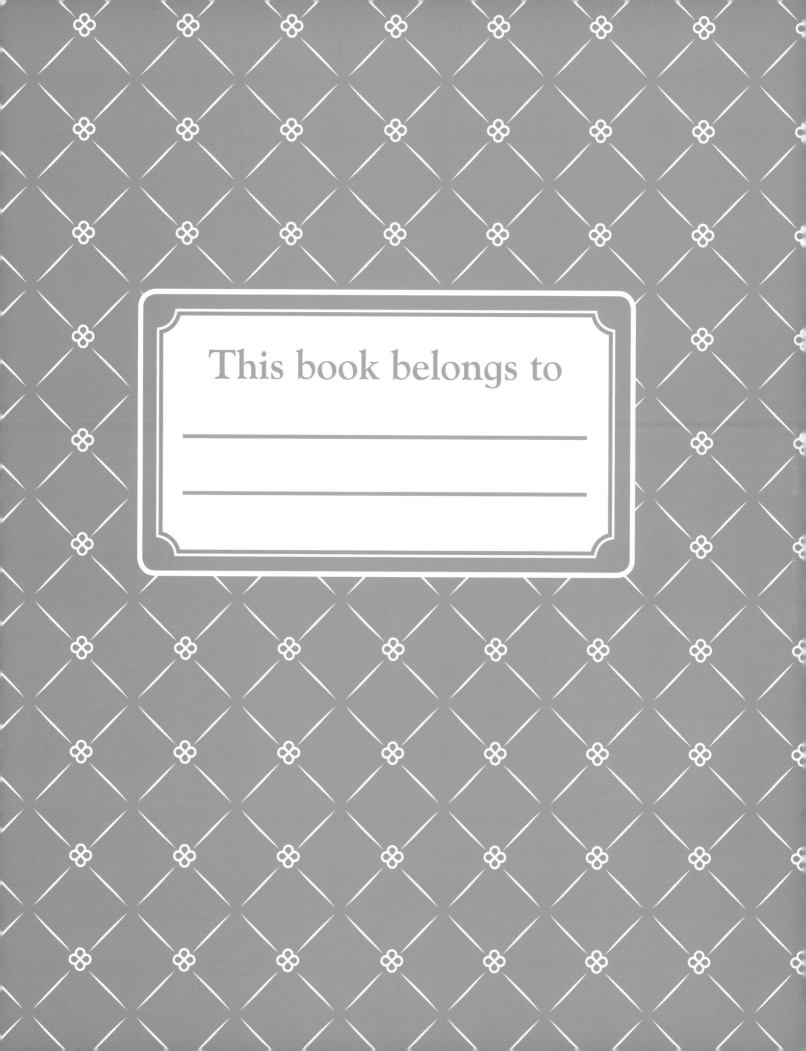

This book belongs to

_____

_____

This edition published by Parragon Books Ltd in 2014

Parragon Books Ltd
Chartist House
15–17 Trim Street
Bath BA1 1HA, UK
www.parragon.com

ISBN 978-1-4723-8198-9

Printed in China

DISNEY MOVIE COLLECTION
A SPECIAL DISNEY STORYBOOK SERIES

THE LITTLE
MERMAID

PaRragon

Bath · New York · Cologne · Melbourne · Delhi
Hong Kong · Shenzhen · Singapore · Amsterdam

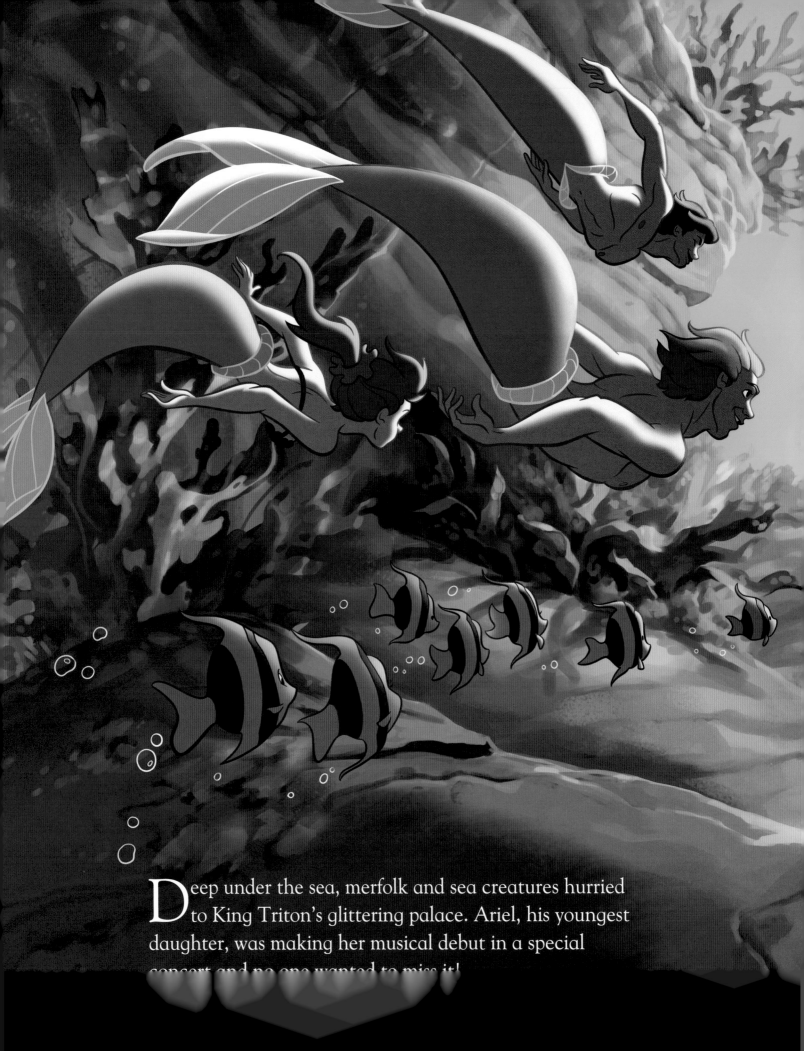

Deep under the sea, merfolk and sea creatures hurried to King Triton's glittering palace. Ariel, his youngest daughter, was making her musical debut in a special concert and no one wanted to miss it!

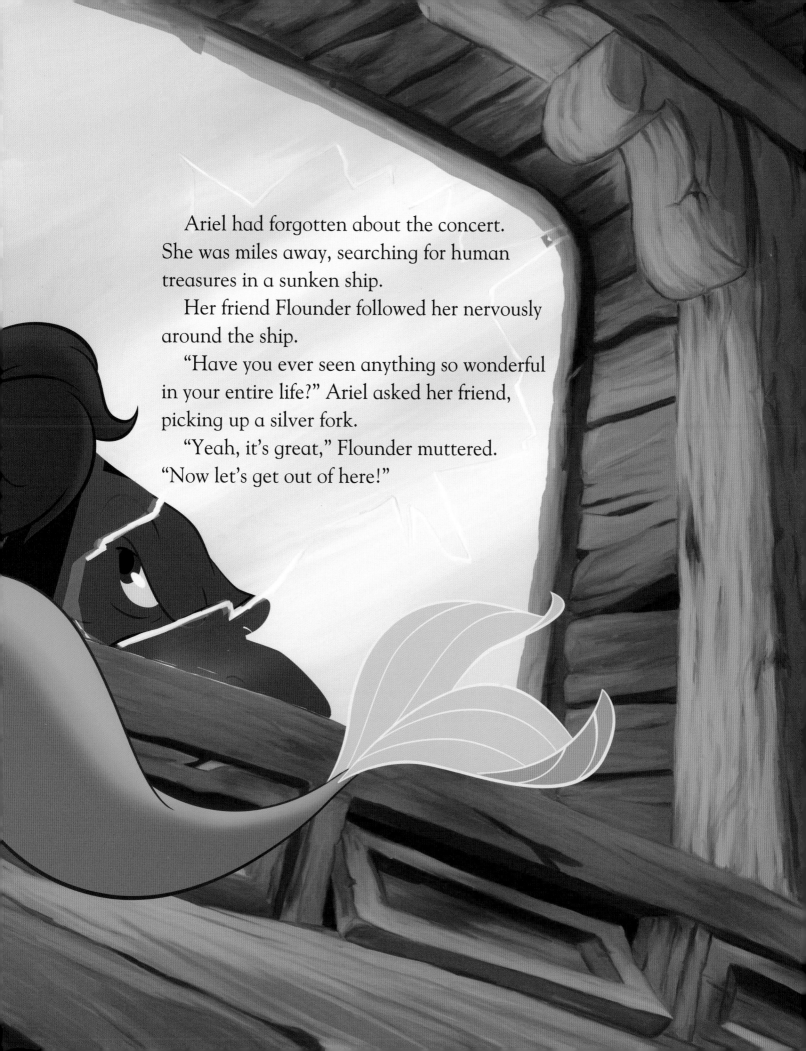

Ariel had forgotten about the concert. She was miles away, searching for human treasures in a sunken ship.

Her friend Flounder followed her nervously around the ship.

"Have you ever seen anything so wonderful in your entire life?" Ariel asked her friend, picking up a silver fork.

"Yeah, it's great," Flounder muttered. "Now let's get out of here!"

Suddenly, a huge mouth of teeth appeared behind them.

"A shark! Swim!" Flounder shouted.

The two friends swam for their lives as the shark charged after them. As the shark leaped forward to take a big bite it got stuck tight in an old anchor.

"Take that, you big bully!" Flounder taunted.

Ariel and Flounder swam to the surface to find Scuttle,
a seagull who claimed to know all about the human world.
Scuttle examined the fork. "This is a dinglehopper,"
he said. "Humans use these to comb their hair."
Just then, Ariel remembered the concert.
"My father's going to kill me!" she gasped.

In a cave, a sea witch called Ursula used her
magic to watch Ariel hurry home.
     She laughed to herself as she thought of her plan
to use Ariel to get back at King Triton.

When King Triton learned that Ariel had missed the concert because she had been to the surface, he was furious. He believed humans were dangerous and he wanted to protect her.

"You are never to go to the surface again!" he commanded.

After Ariel left, King Triton asked Sebastian to keep an eye on her.

Sebastian followed Ariel to a secret grotto. When he peeked inside, he was stunned to see that it was filled with human treasures.

The little crab was shocked to overhear Ariel tell Flounder how much she wanted to be part of the human world.

Sebastian tried to talk some sense into Ariel, but she didn't want to listen. Before he could stop her, Ariel swam to the surface again – to watch a large ship sail past.

King Triton arrived as everyone gathered in
the great hall. With a tap of his baton, Sebastian,
the court composer, instructed the orchestra
to begin. But when the time came to introduce
Ariel ... she wasn't there!

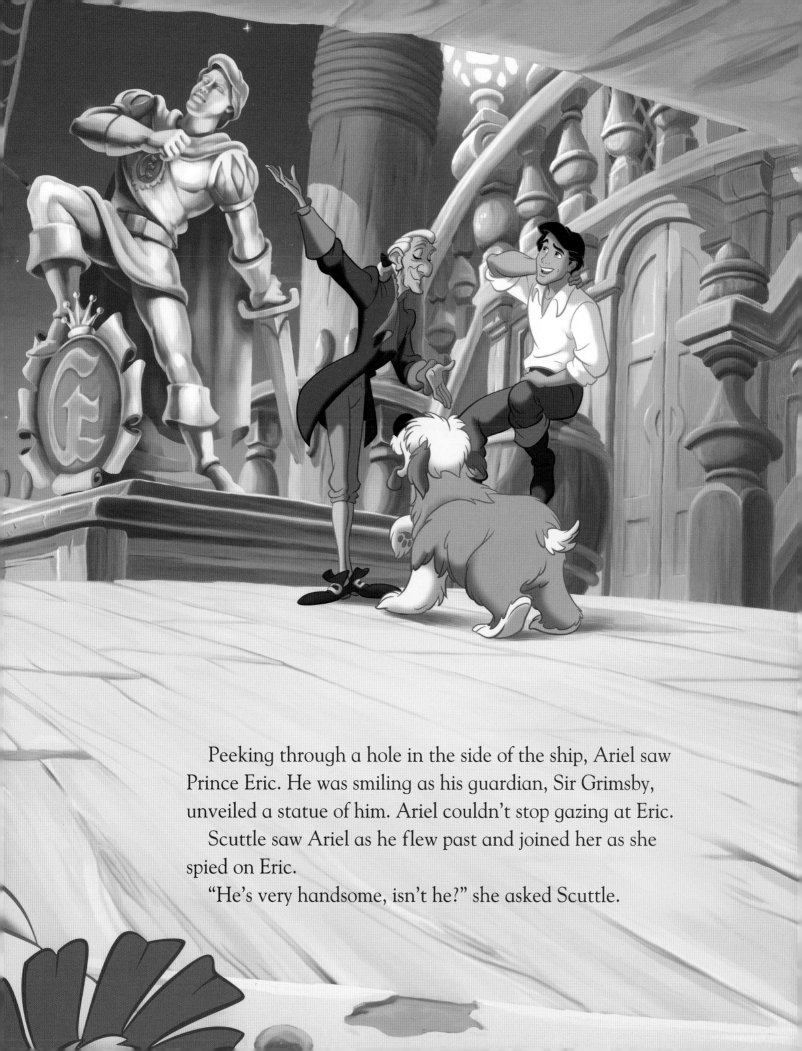

Peeking through a hole in the side of the ship, Ariel saw Prince Eric. He was smiling as his guardian, Sir Grimsby, unveiled a statue of him. Ariel couldn't stop gazing at Eric.

Scuttle saw Ariel as he flew past and joined her as she spied on Eric.

"He's very handsome, isn't he?" she asked Scuttle.

Suddenly, thunder roared and lightning cracked as a storm hit. A lightning bolt struck the ship and set it on fire.

As the fire burned, the ship was rocked by huge waves. Ariel watched in horror as Eric was thrown overboard and swept into the sea.

Beneath the waves, Ariel grabbed the unconscious
prince. Struggling to keep hold of him, she pulled him
to safety on the shore.

While Scuttle listened for a heartbeat, Ariel sang to him in a clear, beautiful voice. But when she heard people approaching she dived quickly back into the sea.

As Eric woke up he only caught a glimpse of her face, but he knew he would never be able to forget her voice.

Ariel was in love and all she could do was think about Eric. Her father noticed her strange behaviour and asked Sebastian to take him to Ariel.

At the entrance of her grotto, King Triton watched as his love-struck daughter sang about a human!

Furious, Triton burst in. "Contact between the human world and merworld is forbidden!"

"But, Daddy, I love him!" announced Ariel.

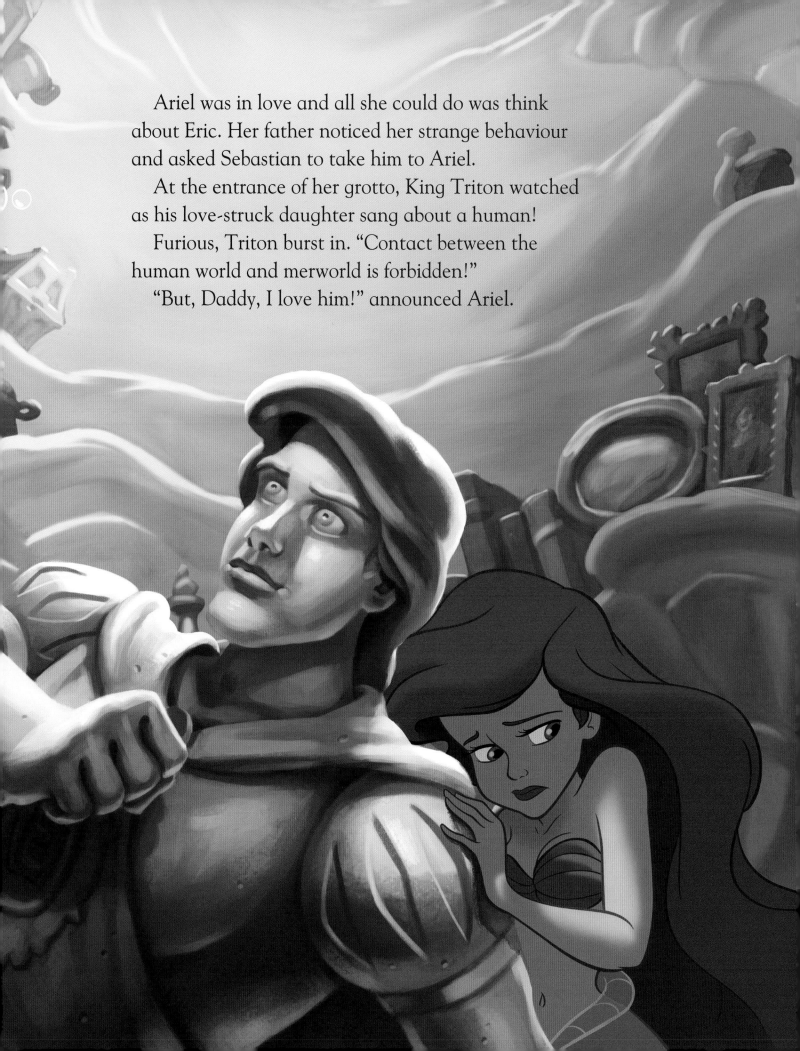

"If this is the only way to get through to you, then so be it!" Triton shouted as he raised his trident.

Flashes of light filled the room and the statue of Eric and the rest of Ariel's treasures were destroyed.

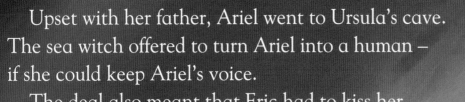

Upset with her father, Ariel went to Ursula's cave.
The sea witch offered to turn Ariel into a human –
if she could keep Ariel's voice.

The deal also meant that Eric had to kiss her
before sunset on the third day.

"If not, you'll turn back into a mermaid
and belong to me!" Ursula cackled.

I hereby grant
unto URSULA, the
Witch of the Sea...
one voice,
in exchange for
byon once high,
Dinu egihn thon
Threo serr'n
Phur-gurr I
reht rasn
retn or m schne
urpl: m srerp
munk gurek, Ch
Eich rloy ri imn
ro mund

for all eternity.
signed,

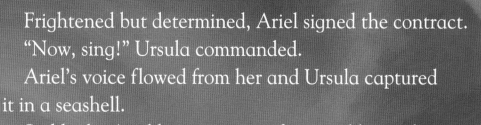

Frightened but determined, Ariel signed the contract.
"Now, sing!" Ursula commanded.
Ariel's voice flowed from her and Ursula captured
it in a seashell.
Suddenly, Ariel began to transform and her tail
disappeared. In its place, she had legs.

Flounder and Sebastian helped Ariel to the surface,
where she looked at her new legs, delighted.
Sebastian was worried about Ariel and agreed to help
her, along with her friends, in the human world.

Just as Ariel's friends helped her to the shore and dressed her in an old ragged sail, the prince and his dog appeared and spotted her.

"You look familiar," Eric told Ariel. Was she the girl who sang to him? But when Eric realized that Ariel couldn't talk, he decided she couldn't be the girl he was looking for.

Eric took Ariel back to his palace where she was dressed
in a beautiful ball gown and invited to dinner.
    To the prince's surprise Ariel combed her hair with a
fork, just as Scuttle had taught her. Sebastian hid himself
at the dinner table so that he could keep an eye on Ariel.

The next day, Eric took Ariel on a tour of his kingdom. Despite the fun they had, Eric still had not kissed her and there was only one day left!

At sunset, the prince took Ariel rowing on a lagoon. Sebastian – with the help of the others – sang a song about love. Eric gazed at Ariel, but just as they were about to kiss the boat was tipped over by eels that had been sent by Ursula.

Ursula used her magic to watch from her cave.

"That was too close," she said to herself. "It's time I took matters into my own hands."

Ursula then transformed herself into a beautiful young woman named Vanessa. She wore a necklace with the shell that contained Ariel's voice.

When Ariel woke up the next day, she rushed
downstairs to see Eric announce his marriage to Vanessa.
Ariel was heartbroken. She had lost her true love and
now she would never escape Ursula's clutches.
"The wedding ship departs at sunset," Eric told Grimsby.

Once aboard the ship Ursula gloated. She had managed to trick the prince using Ariel's beautiful singing voice and had put him under a spell. Soon, Ursula would rule the sea!

Ursula didn't notice that Scuttle had seen her talk about her plan through a porthole. He saw her true reflection in the mirror.

Scuttle flew back to tell Ariel that the girl that the prince was marrying was really Ursula the sea witch in disguise.

They had to stop the wedding! Ariel and her friends hurried to the ship. But the sun was going down. They had to move fast!

The wedding had already started when Ariel and her friends arrived at the ship.

Eric stood in a trance before the minister. Vanessa smiled to herself as they got closer to being married. She was sure that her plan was going to work. Ariel would be hers forever!

But just before Vanessa could say her vows all the
animals that Ariel's friends had rounded up came to the rescue.
Scuttle managed to yank the necklace from Vanessa's neck
and it smashed on the floor. Ariel's voice flowed back to her and
Eric was released from the spell.

"You're the one!" exclaimed Eric as he heard Ariel's voice.

"You're too late!" laughed Ursula. The sun had set beneath the horizon and Ariel became a mermaid again. Ursula changed back into her real form as the sea witch and dragged Ariel into the sea.

"I'm not going to lose her again!" shouted Eric as he went after Ariel.

Beneath the sea, King Triton appeared. "Ursula! Let her go!"
"She's mine now," Ursula replied, showing him Ariel's contract.
"We made a deal – but I might be willing to make an exchange."

To save his beloved daughter, Triton agreed to take Ariel's place. Now he would be Ursula's servant forever!

Ursula took the king's trident and stirred the waves, creating a huge whirlpool.

"Now I'm the ruler of the all the ocean!" she declared as Ariel and Eric watched in horror.

Ursula grew and grew until she towered over
the sea.

Eric saw an ancient sunken ship rising through
the whirlpool and decided to climb aboard.

Just as Ursula took aim at him with her fiery trident
he steered the jagged bow through the sea witch's heart.

The sea witch disappeared beneath the waves –
her spell was broken. King Triton and all the poor,
unfortunate souls Ursula had tricked were free at last!

But Ariel was a mermaid and Eric would always be a human. King Triton watched his daughter gaze longingly at her true love on the shore.

With a sigh, he touched his trident to the water and turned Ariel back into a human. The king smiled tenderly as he watched Ariel walk out of the sea to be with her one true love.

Some time later, Ariel's friends and family gathered to watch Ariel and Prince Eric get married. At last, she was part of the human world she loved. And she would live there happily ever after.